THIS

SWEET PICKLES ®

BOOK
BELONGS TO

James R. Smith

Taska

In the world of *Sweet Pickles,* each animal gets into a pickle because of an all too human personality trait.

This book is about Smarty Stork. He has answers for every question, including who delivers babies.

Other Books in the Sweet Pickles Series

ME TOO IGUANA
ZEBRA ZIPS BY
GOOSE GOOFS OFF
VERY WORRIED WALRUS
FIXED BY CAMEL

Library of Congress Cataloging in Publication Data

Hefter, Richard.
  Stork spills the beans.

  (Sweet Pickles series)
  SUMMARY: Stork sets the residents of Sweet Pickles
straight about what he does and doesn't deliver.
  [1. Storks–Fiction] I. Title. II. Series.
PZ7.H3587Sr   [E]   76-44020
ISBN 0-03-018076-7

Printed in the United States of America

Weekly Reader Books' Edition

Weekly Reader Books presents

STORK
SPILLS
THE BEANS

Written and Illustrated
by Richard Hefter

Edited by Ruth Lerner Perle

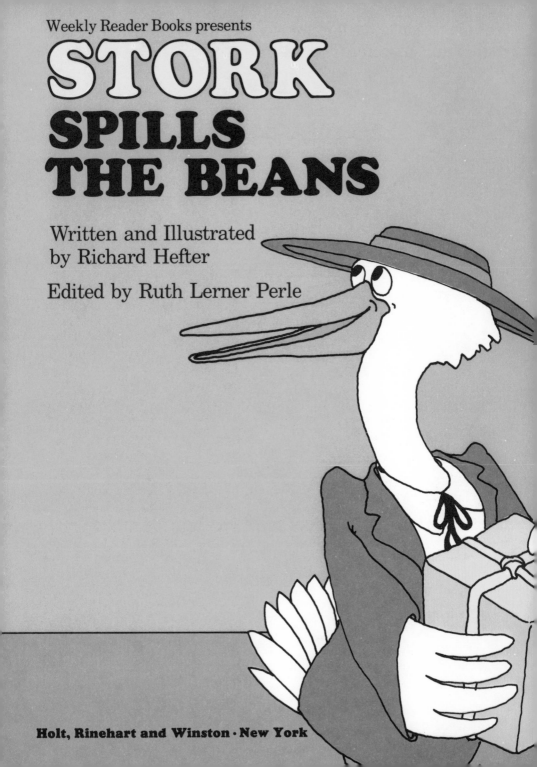

Holt, Rinehart and Winston · New York

One day, Lion and Alligator were sitting around in the park talking about things.

"I wonder where babies come from," said Lion.
"That's easy," Alligator replied. "They come from under a cabbage leaf."

"That's the silliest thing I ever heard," laughed Lion. "Babies do not come from under a cabbage leaf…it's impossible. It's damp and dirty under cabbage leaves and everyone knows you have to keep babies clean and dry."

"All right, wise guy," squealed Alligator. "If they don't come from under a cabbage leaf, where *do* they come from?"

"I don't know for sure," said Lion, scratching his mane, but I do know that you won't find babies under the cabbage, or the lettuce, or the carrot plants or anywhere else in the garden."

"Well, you're wrong," said Alligator. "Babies come from under cabbage leaves."

"They do not," giggled Lion.
"Do so!" shouted Alligator.

"DO NOT!"
"DO SO!"
"DO NOT!"
"DO SO!"

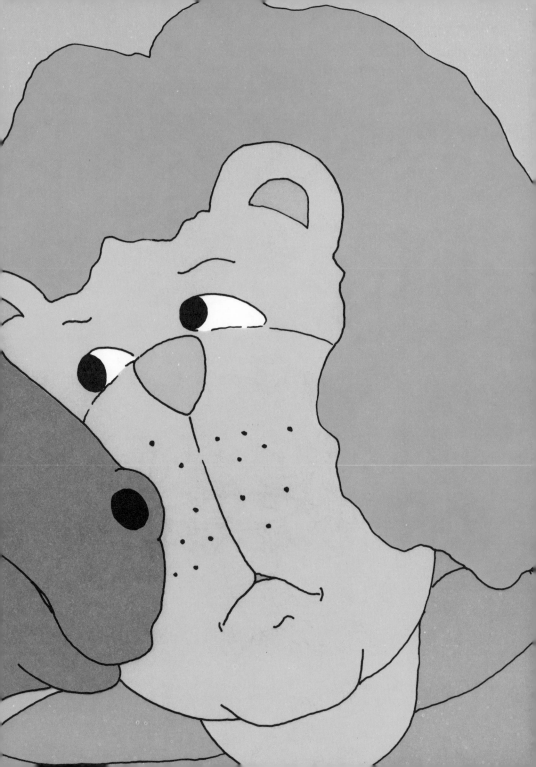

Just then, Elephant passed the bench where Lion and Alligator were arguing. "Hold on there," she said. "What are you two fighting about?"

"This silly Alligator," said Lion, "just told me that babies come from under cabbage leaves. Have you ever heard anything so funny?"

Elephant laughed and said, "Where do *you* think babies come from, Lion?"

"I don't know for sure," admitted Lion, "but I know it's not from under a leaf."

"No, it isn't," agreed Elephant. "*I* can tell you where babies come from."

Lion and Alligator looked at Elephant.
"Well?" they both asked.

"Babies," Elephant said, "are brought by Stork. Stork delivers babies."

"YES!" said Lion. "Of course! That's right! That's it! Stork delivers babies. After all, he's the postmaster."

"I still think they come from under cabbage leaves, and you can't tell me that Stork delivers them!" roared Alligator.

"Well, there's only one way to make sure," said Elephant. "Let's go to the post office and ask Stork. Then you will know for sure."

They all left the park and went across the street to the post office.

In the post office, they found Stork busily stacking packages.

"Stork," they all said at once, "we have a question."

"Hold on there," said Stork. "One at a time! I'm always happy to answer questions, and I have an answer for every question. But you will have to ask them one at a time 'cause I can't answer two at a time."

"Stork," said Lion, "Alligator says that babies come from under a cabbage leaf."

"No, they don't," said Stork. "But I can tell you about a carload of cabbage leaves I sent to a rabbit in Memphis once. I remember it very well. It was July and very hot. Those leaves were heavy, too. I had to put them on special delivery so they wouldn't spoil."

"Wait a minute, Stork," Elephant trumpeted. "That wasn't the question."

"Well, what was it then?" asked Stork. "Sounded like a question to me."

Elephant said, "The question is–Stork, do you deliver babies?"

Stork stood up on a box. "Ah, ahem, yes, well, I've been asked that before. And the answer is pretty easy. I've delivered boxes of letters and soft, fuzzy sweaters, refrigerators, percolators, radiators and ventilators. I've brought lemonade and marmalade, lampshades, spades and ropes in braids. I've delivered bags of flags and boxes with tags, envelopes and cantaloupes, kaleidoscopes and antelopes. I've delivered 'most everything…balloons and spoons and hairy baboons, hats and bats and coats for cats, snakes and flakes and wedding cakes. Everything comes through the post office! As postmaster, I deliver airplanes, canes and weather vanes. But I *don't* deliver babies!"

"You don't?" exclaimed Alligator.

"You don't bring them?" cried Lion.

"If it's not you," said Elephant, "where *do* babies come from?"

"Well," said Stork, "it's really very simple. I can tell you in one word where babies come from."

"I know, I know," said Alligator. "The word is store."
"Nope," said Stork.

"I know, I know," said Lion. "The word is Mars. Babies come from Mars."

"Nope," said Stork.

"Well, where *do* babies come from?" sighed Lion. "Will we ever find out?"

"Yep," said Stork, "I'll tell you right now."

"Babies come from MOTHERS.

"Yes, they do."

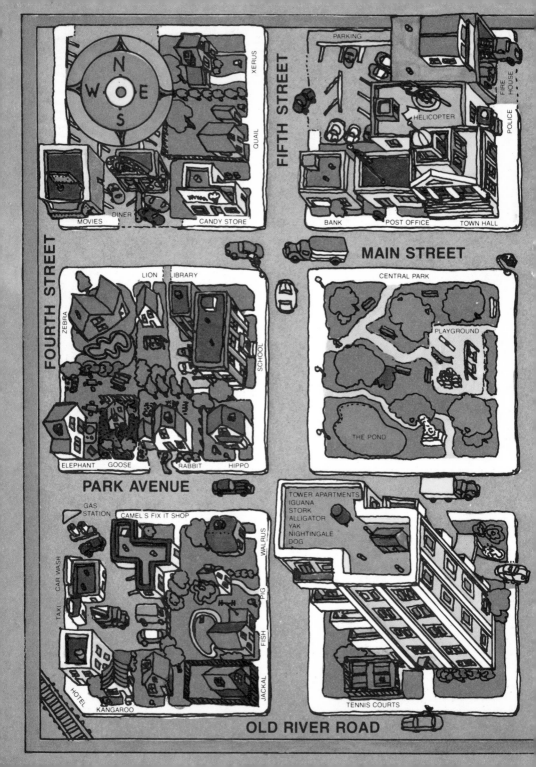